LIVERWURST IS MISSING

LIVERWURST IS MISSING

by Mercer Mayer
illustrated by Steven Kellogg

Morrow Junior Books · New York

Printed in the United States of America.
2 3 4 5 6 7 8 9 10
Library of Congress Cataloging-in-Publication Data
Mayer, Mercer, 1943-
Liverwurst is missing / by Mercer Mayer ; illustrated by Steven Kellogg.
p. cm.
Summary: When Liverwurst the baby rhinosterwurst disappears,
Wackatoo Indians, survivors of the 49th Cavalry, and children from
the Koala Scouts join the circus company in rescuing him from a
burger tycoon interested in creating Rhino-burgers.
ISBN 0-688-09657-3. — ISBN 0-688-09658-1 (lib. bdg.)
[1. Kidnapping—Fiction.] I. Kellogg, Steven, ill. II. Title.
PZ7.M462Lhp 1990
[E]—dc20   90-5434   CIP   AC

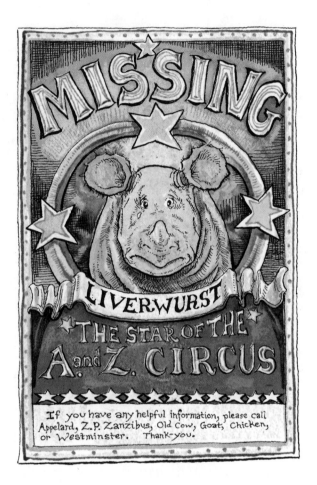

To Steve and Helen,
and the whole wonderful Kellogg brood
M.M.

To the Mayer family
S.K.

Ａll aboard," called the conductor. The Zanzibus Circus was leaving town, and everything was all packed and ready to go.

"Wait," called Appelard. "Liverwurst is missing!" Everyone on the train gasped. Liverwurst, the baby rhinosterwurst, was the star of the show!

"Moo," said the old cow.

"Pluck, pluck," said the chicken.

"Grunt," said Westminster the pig, and all the billy goat did was spit. They were Liverwurst's best friends.

Sure enough, Liverwurst's private car was empty. His
mother was asleep in the next car. "Oh, dear," said Appelard.
"We'd better find him before his mother notices he's missing."

Appelard noticed a mushroom lying just outside of the
door of Liverwurst's car. Mushrooms were Liverwurst's very fa-
vorite food. "Someone has led him away with mushrooms—
see, there's his trail," said Appelard. "The rest of you go on
ahead, and we'll stay behind and find him."

The train tooted and disappeared down the tracks.

"Something terrible must have happened," said Appelard.
"Why would anyone want to lead Liverwurst away?"

They tracked Liverwurst through Bovine Junction where
they were spotted by the burger tycoon Archibald McDoot III,
who owned half the town.

"Stray animals are bad for business," he grumbled. "If they
weren't such miserable specimens I'd ship them to my factory
and turn them into hamburgers."

Instead he lodged a complaint, and Appelard was given
a summons for letting his animals walk through a public place.

Appelard told his story to the judge, who immediately began to weep when he remembered losing his pet kitten as a child. He then gave Appelard a permit allowing him and his animals to roam wherever they pleased in search of Liverwurst.

The trail led them out of town and into a woodland where they came upon Chief Sorefoot and a band of Wackatoo Indians. The chief told Appelard that they had escaped from the Asphalt Flats Reservation. They had been forced to settle there after Archibald McDoot III had taken over all the forests in the county.

"We're tired of that reservation!" declared the chief. "We're looking for some adventure!"

Appelard told them of Liverwurst's plight. Never having seen a rhinosterwurst before, Chief Sorefoot and his braves offered to join the search party.

They followed the trail to McDoot's Burger Palace where it gave out. Chief Sorefoot, a keen tracker, noticed that a vehicle carrying something very heavy had driven off down Old Skeeterbrook Road. "Liverwurst must have been taken by truck!" he cried. Off they all ran in pursuit.

Old Skeeterbrook Road passed right in front of the Grimmdale Old Folks' Home where all four survivors of the 49th Cavalry were living. As Appelard and his friends came down the road, General Bluster N. Finbee exclaimed, "Egads—the Wack-atoos are on the warpath again!" He pulled his rusty old bugle out of his army trunk and gave it a loud blast. Immediately the members of the 49th fell into attention in full uniform. Barking orders, General Finbee and his men set off down the road after the Indians.

"It's all over!" announced Finbee in a shrill voice. "You're surrounded on all sides! There's no way out but peaceful surrender!"

When Appelard and the Indians calmed him down and explained what was going on, Finbee and the rest of the cavalry voted to abandon the old folks' home and to join ranks with Appelard and his friends. They all pushed on in search of Liverwurst.

Their route took them near Camp Wattalottafun. Head Counselor Bloombritches and the campers stood sadly beside their tent, which was surrounded by tree stumps.

"Who chopped down all these trees?" asked Appelard.

"The woods were bought last month by the Archibald McDoot Burger Works," wailed Ms. Bloombritches. "And since then they've destroyed everything. EVERYTHING! We've been given one week to pack up and ship out!"

"McDoot uses the sawdust from the trees in his burger buns," grumbled Chief Sorefoot.

Seeing the animals, the Indian braves, and the soldiers raised the spirits of the children, and they begged Ms. Bloombritches to let them join the search for Liverwurst. She brightened at the thought, blew a wild blast on her whistle, and cried, "ALL RIGHT, KOALA SCOUTS! PACK UP FOR AN OVERNIGHTER AND LET'S GO!"

Late that afternoon the trail ended at the front gates of Bleakwood Manor, the estate of Archibald McDoot III.

"What can *he* want with Liverwurst?" asked Appelard. "We'd better hurry."

A scouting party crept over the wall and made its way toward the mansion.

Chief Sorefoot froze under a window when he heard a voice saying, "Is this the Gallows Butcher Company? Good. This is Archibald McDoot III. My men have the rhinoceros. Send the truck in the morning, and, when you're finished, deliver the meat to my factory. Soon I'll be famous with the first Rhinoburgers in the world!"

"Oh, mercy," whispered the chief, and he crawled away to tell Appelard what he'd overheard.

They searched the estate until they found Liverwurst in a basement room, where he was being held prisoner by Archibald McDoot's bodyguards.

Appelard had a plan, and he made a long distance telephone call to the circus.

When Z.P. Zanzibus, the ringmaster, hung up, he rented an airplane and coaxed Liverwurst's mother aboard.

Before dawn she was dropped into the woods near Bleakwood Manor, where Appelard and his friends were waiting.

As the first rays of the morning sun crept across the hills, the butcher's truck came rumbling down the road. Liverwurst's mother blocked its way and bellowed an angry challenge. The driver slammed on his brakes, leaped from the cab, and ran.

"We'll take over from here," said Appelard. He jumped into the truck, while the others took their places in the shrubbery around the estate.

When Appelard arrived at the mansion, Archibald McDoot and his bodyguards were there with Liverwurst.

"Are you ready, butcher?" asked the tycoon.

"More ready than you could guess!" answered Appelard.

He opened the rear of the truck, and Liverwurst's mother charged forward to rescue her baby.

Archibald McDoot and his bodyguards fled to the garage.

But several moments later they emerged heavily armed. "ARCHIBALD McDOOT III NEVER SURRENDERS!" thundered the tycoon.

Liverwurst hid in a rose trellis, but his mother positioned herself in front of the swimming pool and turned to face her enemy.

She stood her ground until the tank was almost upon her, and then, at the last possible moment, she stepped aside, and the ponderous machine, unable to swerve quickly enough, hurtled past her into the pool.

Ms. Bloombritches, from her lookout post atop an elm, blew a signal on her whistle that meant "troops assemble!" Meanwhile Appelard telephoned the constable.

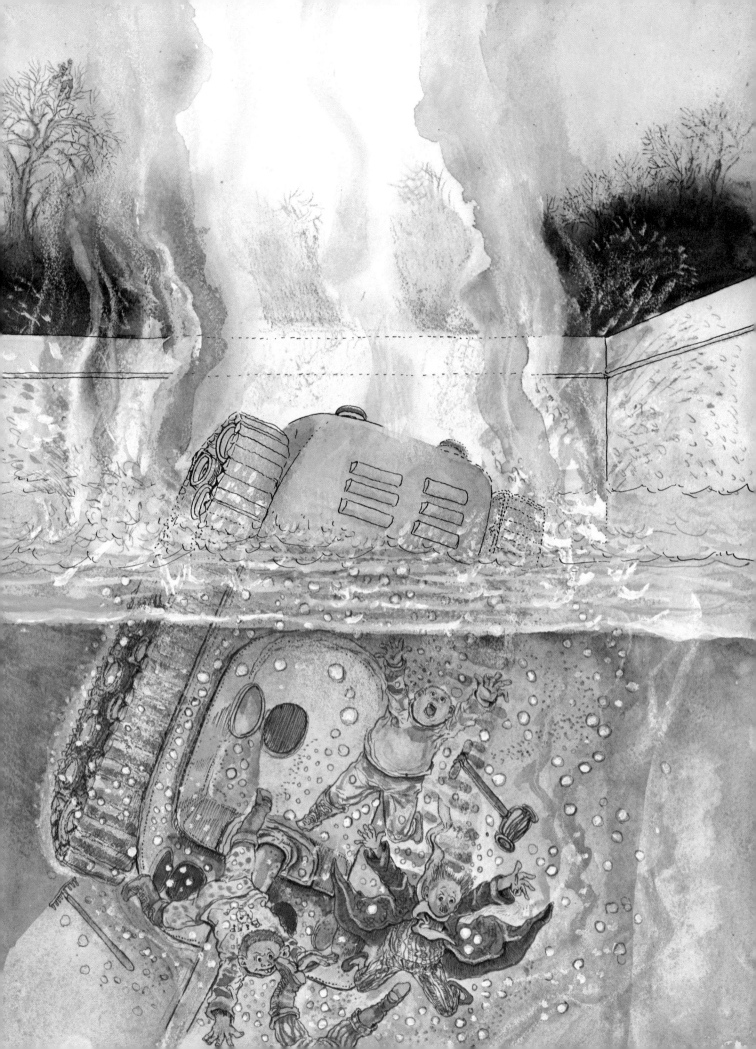

As soon as Archibald McDoot and his soaked and ex-hausted bodyguards had escaped from beneath the sunken tank and dragged themselves out of the pool, they were pounced upon by the Indian braves, the 49th Cavalry, the animals, the Koala Scouts, and Appelard.

When the judge heard about Archibald McDoot's dastardly deeds, he gave him a stern lecture and threatened to lock him up forever. McDoot trembled, said he was sorry, and promised to make up for being so bad.

He gave his mansion to the old folks, turned the grounds of the estate into a wonderful camp for the Koala Scouts, and gave the entire forest back to the Indians. Then he sold his burger factories and franchises and bought the Northern Mississippi Maulers, a famous professional football club. His bodyguards eagerly signed up for the team, and the next day they took off to play their first game.

Before Appelard and the other animals got back on the train, they invited the rest of the circus to join the Wackatoos, the Koalas, and the 49th Cavalry in a Wild West revue and carnival. When the word got out, all the townspeople showed up, too, and it was the best party in the history of Bovine Junction.

The End